The Birth of the Mysterious Mustache

Written by Zachary A. Schaefer
Illustrated by Elizabeth Gearhart
Designed by Zachary A. Schaefer

Published by *CommSolver Press*, an imprint of
Mediation and Communication Solutions, LLC.

The Birth of the Mysterious Mustache

By Zachary A. Schaefer
&
Illustrated by Elizabeth Gearhart

Dedication

To humans who inspire others to go *beyond*...

On a pleasing fall evening,
So crisp you could see yourself breathing,
Allen and Elizabeth skipped along the air so chilly,
Having fun and acting quite silly.

They were visiting the Arch in front of the Mighty Mississippi,
It's the Gateway to the West and looks really nifty.

Before they journeyed up a unique elevator ride,
Their mouths were drooling and their eyes were wide,
As they stared at a cart with foods that were fried.

After wiping off the mustard and drinking a hot tea,
They headed to the top of the Arch to see what they could see.

The elevator stopped in front of three tiny windows.
Elizabeth smiled at the breathtaking views,
"The sunlight is glistening with gorgeous hues."

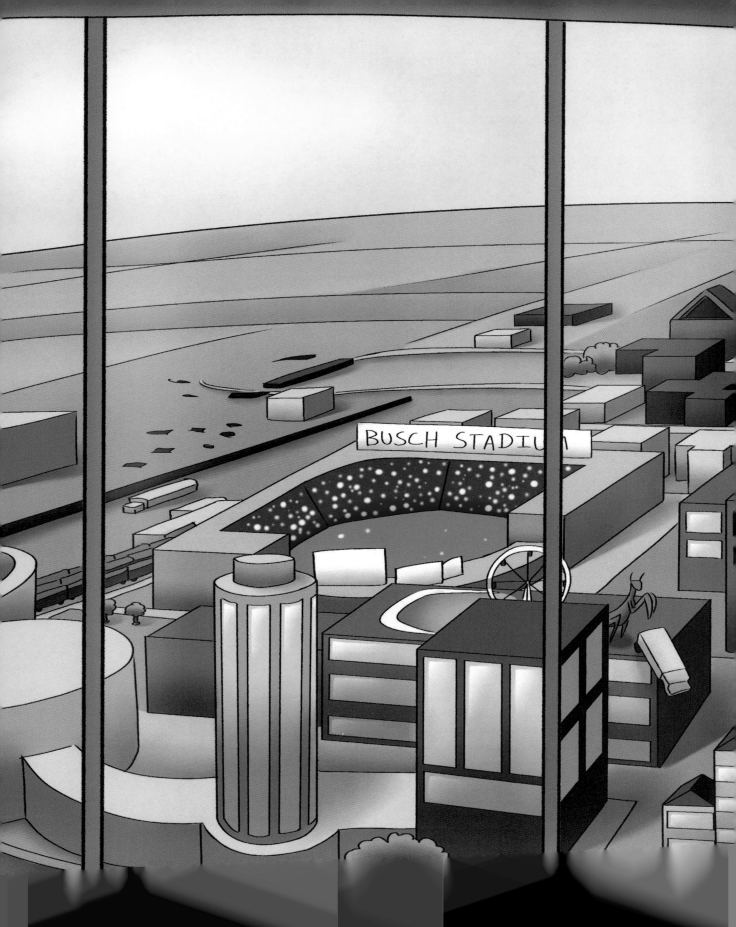

The home team was teaching a lesson in winning,
The scoreboard said 7–0, and it was the 9th inning!

The fans were on their feet,
swaying side-to-side,
As Elizabeth exclaimed,
"That's Red Bird Pride."

After taking in views of the city and game,
They headed to the aquarium for which they came.

They ran into old friends named Kizzy and Zach,
Who were playing with ducks, and saying, "Quack. Quack."

To Allen and Elizabeth's surprise,
They had a baby girl with beautiful hazel eyes.

"Her name is Claudia," said Kizzy with a grin.
"She's sure to be loved by all of our friends."

The group made good time to the front of the line,
But were greeted by an eye that appeared unkind.

"Did we make it in time?"
The Cyclops cashier acted like they committed a crime,
As she painfully pointed to a large yellow sign.

"Whew," said Allen as he wiped his brow,
"Only FIVE minutes to spare. Holy cow!"

They hurried past the shark tanks and dolphin displays,
The king-size stingrays never caught their gaze.
They wanted to see the enormous and flawless
Wallace the Walrus.

To get a good look at Wallace's mass,
Elizabeth pressed her face against the cold glass.
She soon caught Wallace's attention,
And he began to swim very fast.

Once the beast spotted the group his speed decreased.
Because he smelled the aroma of his evening feast.

Before Wallace scarfed his evening meal,
He kissed the glass near Elizabeth's belly
And let out a giant walrus squeal.

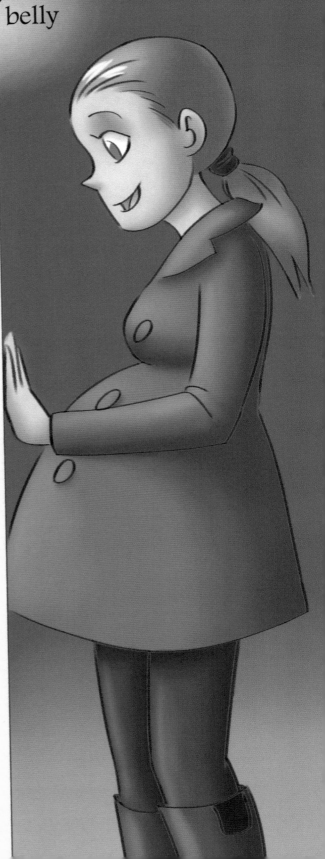

Elizabeth knew that this lucky sign
Would leave their son with something divine.

Made in the USA
Charleston, SC
13 August 2015